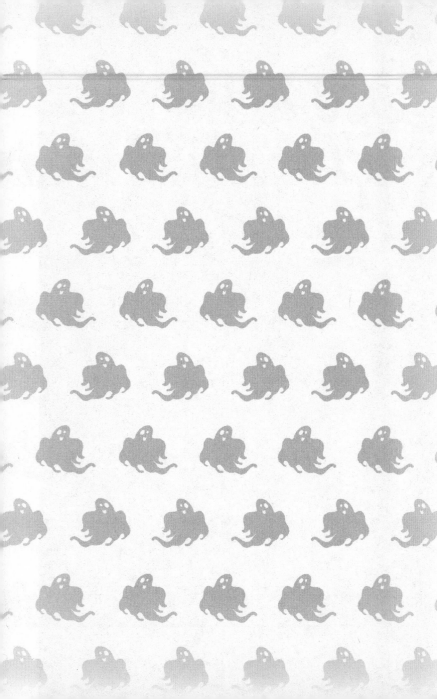

DESMOND COLE
GHOST PATROL

BEWARE THE WEREWOLF

by Andres Miedoso
illustrated by Victor Rivas

LITTLE SIMON

New York   London   Toronto   Sydney   New Delhi

LITTLE SIMON
An imprint of
Simon & Schuster Children's Publishing Division
1230 Avenue of the Americas, New York, New York 10020
First Little Simon hardcover edition October 2020
Copyright © 2020 by Simon & Schuster, Inc.
Also available in a Little Simon paperback edition.
All rights reserved, including the right of reproduction
in whole or in part in any form.
LITTLE SIMON is a registered trademark of Simon & Schuster, Inc.,
and associated colophon is a trademark of Simon & Schuster, Inc.
For information about special discounts for bulk purchases, please contact
Simon & Schuster Special Sales at 1-866-506-1949 or
business@simonandschuster.com.
The Simon & Schuster Speakers Bureau can bring authors to your
live event. For more information or to book an event contact the
Simon & Schuster Speakers Bureau at 1-866-248-3049
or visit our website at www.simonspeakers.com.
Designed by Steve Scott
Manufactured in the United States of America 0920 FFG
2 4 6 8 10 9 7 5 3 1
This book has been cataloged with the Library of Congress.
ISBN 978-1-5344-7956-2 (hc)
ISBN 978-1-5344-7955-5 (pbk)
ISBN 978-1-5344-7957-9 (eBook)

CONTENTS

CHAPTER ONE

ALL BARK, NO BITE

There are two kinds of people in the world. There are dog people, and there are cat people. If I have to pick, I guess I would say I, Andres Miedoso, am a cat person.

I mean, cats are just the coolest, aren't they?

They spend all day eating, sleeping, and relaxing. It's like their whole life is a summer vacation!

Not only that—cats don't need to be walked. They go to the bathroom by themselves. *In private!* Sure, you have to scoop it up, but I would rather clean a litter box than pick up doggy doo.

Yuck!

Dogs are the exact opposite. They need your attention. *All. The. Time.* Sheesh.

Dogs need you to walk them, pet them, and play with them. It's like they don't understand that sometimes you just want to sit and read and not have a wet nose poking you.

I mean, is that too much to ask?

My best friend, Desmond Cole, is a dog person through and through. That boy is crazy about dogs. He's always walking up to dog owners to ask a million questions about their dogs.

Then
he has to
pet their
dogs. And
that leads to
him hugging their dogs.
And then he's playing with their dogs.

    I've had to drag him away from
other people's dogs so many times.

Desmond tells me he wants to have his own dog, but he can't. His mom and dad are allergic. They sneeze, wheeze, itch, and scratch like they are the ones with fleas! No way can they have a dog in their house.

But that doesn't stop Desmond
from falling in love with every single
pup he sees.

Maybe that explains why Desmond and I are outside in the middle of the night, under a full moon. And why we're dressed like giant cats, running from a pack of dogs, including the largest dog either of us has ever seen.

But none of this will make sense unless I go back and start at the beginning. Way back to . . . yesterday.

CHAPTER TWO

PUPPY LOVE

It was a sunny day, and Desmond and I were at Kersville Park. Desmond was looking for ghosts, because he's always looking for ghosts. Not me, though. I was looking for the last ice-cream truck before the weather turned too cold.

I mean, it's not like kids stop wanting ice cream for eight months out of the year!

Anyway, we were walking through the park, minding our own business, when a creepy creature leaped out of the bushes.

"Aaarrgh!" I screamed. "You found a ghost!"

My feet started running away before the rest of my body.

"Relax, Andres," Desmond called out, smiling. "It's just a puppy."

I stopped running and stared at the little thing. It *was* just a puppy, but, boy, it was the ugliest puppy I'd ever seen.

He was all scruffy and shaggy. His teeth were snaggy, and his tail was scrawny. There was something *really* strange about this dog.

That didn't stop Desmond, though. He loved dogs no matter how ugly they were. Desmond bent down to pet him.

"Be careful," I warned. "That dog looks haunted. In fact, maybe he's not a dog at all! Maybe he's a baby monster, which means there could be a monster family in the park!"

"Don't be silly," Desmond said, standing up. "Let me check." He pulled out one of his contraptions.

Seriously, I have no idea where he keeps those things!

Desmond scanned the evil-looking animal, and we both waited as the little machine beeped and dinged.

"Nothing to worry about here," Desmond declared, reading the screen. "See, he's not a monster or a haunted puppy. He's just a dog."

"An ugly dog," I responded. But I was relieved. This is Kersville after all. Anything was possible here. Even a haunted puppy!

Desmond crouched closer to him. "Oh, he's not ugly," he said. "And look how friendly he is." Desmond held out his hand, and the puppy's tail wagged happily. The dog moved closer, but then, just like that, he took off running.

And then, just like that, Desmond chased after him!

And yeah, I chased after Desmond. I mean, what was I supposed to do? Stand there while a monster family might be nearby?

The dog ran under a park bench. Desmond jumped over it. I went around it.

The dog ran up the seesaw and down the other side. Desmond got on the next one, and I hopped on behind him. We balanced ourselves on the way up, but that didn't work on the way down!

Whoops!

Desmond and I fell into a heap on the ground.

And the puppy—he was way ahead of us. He bolted right through a group of people practicing yoga in the park. In just a second, the group went from quiet and calm to angry and shrieking.

See! I wasn't the only one who thought the puppy was a monster.

Desmond kept after him, running right through the group. I went around them because I didn't want to get the yoga people even madder.

"Hurry up!" Desmond screamed. "He's getting away!"

I had no idea why we were chasing the puppy. What did Desmond want with him anyway? He couldn't bring the dog home. Nobody wants to live with sneezy, wheezy parents!

As the dog headed toward the edge of the park, I lost sight of him for a few seconds. Desmond and I ran harder and faster. Then we spotted him and stopped in our tracks, breathing heavily.

"Oh no," Desmond whispered. "This is terrible!"

Right there in front of us, the little puppy was in the arms of a man in a purple uniform. Desmond's little puppy had been nabbed by a city dogcatcher!

CHAPTER THREE

THE DOGCATCHER

"Hey, Mr. Dogcatcher," Desmond began. "Please don't take that puppy!"

We stood there watching as the puppy licked the dogcatcher's face. If we didn't know any better, we would have thought the dogcatcher was his owner.

"Is this your dog?" the dogcatcher asked.

"Um, no," Desmond said. "He's a stray, but I'm going to help him find a home. I'm really good with dogs."

The dogcatcher shook his head. "Sorry, kid," he said. "This dog doesn't have a collar, so it's my job to bring him down to the pound."

He went over to his van and opened the back door. We couldn't believe what we saw. His van was packed full of dogs!

They were all sizes, shapes, and colors, but that wasn't the weird part. I mean, you expect to see dogs in a dogcatcher's van. But these dogs were totally chill and happy.

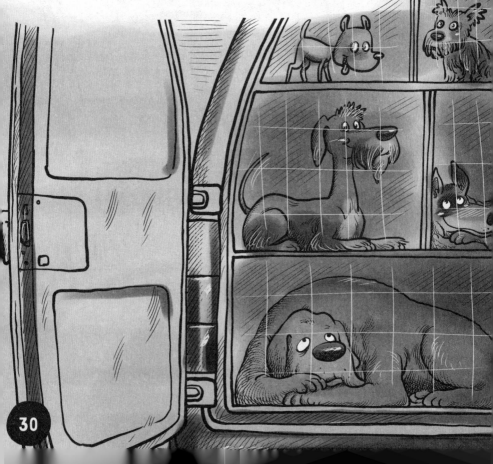

Some of them were even sleeping in their cages!

"That's a lot of strays," Desmond said.

The dogcatcher nodded.

"There's supposed to be a full moon this evening," he said. "Full moons always bring out the dogs. We're going to have a full house down at the pound."

I couldn't be sure, but I thought I saw a little smile on his lips.

The dogcatcher put the little puppy in the van and closed the door. "If you want to visit your pooch," he said, "come to the pound tomorrow. Tonight, he's mine."

As the van drove away, Desmond had a strange look on his face.

"Something weird is going on," he said. "I've never seen a dog *that* happy to be caught by a dogcatcher."

"I know," I responded. "And why were the dogs in the van so calm? It's like they were under a spell."

Desmond shook his head. "I don't know, but we have to find out. We need to make sure that little puppy is going to be safe!"

I could tell Desmond was already making plans.

"Come on, Andres," he said. "We have a dog to rescue!"

CHAPTER FOUR

FREE PUPPIES

Back at my house, Desmond asked my parents if he could use our new family computer.

"It's for a project," he said.

I guess it wasn't a lie. Desmond *was* working on a project—a puppy jailbreak project!

"Of course," Mom told him. "Our computer is your computer."

Desmond and I went into the den.

"We need a plan," he said. "We have to figure out how to get that little puppy—and maybe *all* those dogs—out of the pound. And we need to see if that dogcatcher is haunted."

I could feel a lump form in my throat. "You think the dogcatcher is haunted?"

"You said it yourself, Andres," Desmond reminded me. "Those dogs looked like they were under a spell."

I thought about it, and Desmond was right. There was something odd about seeing dogs acting like cats.

It's like spotting an ice-cream truck parked on the street, without anyone inside it to serve you ice cream. It's just plain *wrong*!

"What can we do?" I asked.

Desmond started typing. "First, let's find the address to the pound."

We waited as the information popped up on the screen.

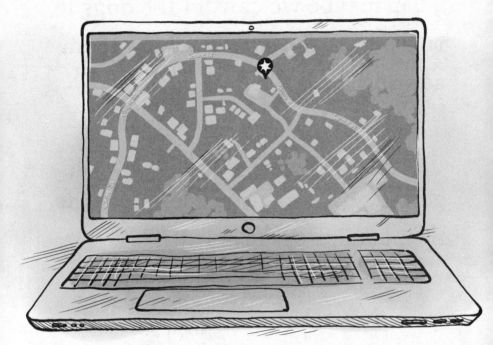

I pointed to the digital map. "It's on Canine Street. That's not far from here."

"Perfect," Desmond said. "Now we need to find something dogs love. Then maybe we can get the dogs to run out of the pound all by themselves."

Desmond always had a plan!

"What about a big ball?" I suggested. "We can bounce it outside the pound. Dogs love balls!"

Desmond shook his head hard. "Remember what happened the last time you played with a big ball?"

I thought back to the big ball disaster. Desmond and I were at the beach playing with a big beach ball. He threw it to me, but I didn't catch it.

Instead, it hit me in the stomach and knocked me over.

Then the ball—and me!—went rolling across the sand dunes, with the wind picking up speed. Round and round I tumbled. It felt like I was stuck in a clothes dryer!

Desmond ran after me, and by the time he caught up, I was very dizzy . . . and very, very sandy!

"Forget about balls," I said. "Dogs like chewing on shoes. Maybe we can bring all our shoes to the pound, and when the dogs see them, they'll race out of there."

"No way!" Desmond said, shaking his head again. "If we let a bunch of dogs chew on our shoes, our parents will make us go shoe shopping. And that's the worst!"

We were both stumped. We had to free those dogs, but how?

"I got it!" Desmond declared. "We can get a couple of cats to hang around outside the pound. When the dogs see the cats, they will *have* to chase them, right?"

I was quiet. I didn't want to poke holes in Desmond's plan, but I knew enough about cats to know there was no way anyone could get cats to do *anything*. That was what made them cats!

And cats would never ever want to hang around a pound and wait to be chased by a pack of dogs. That would be way too scary for the cats!

"Listen," I said. "The only way we could get cats to do what we want would be if we dressed up in cat costumes and let the dogs chase *us*!"

Then I laughed because I was making a joke.

But Desmond didn't laugh. In fact, his eyes lit up, and I knew I had made a huge mistake.

I never should have opened my big mouth!

CHAPTER FIVE

FULL MOON-STER!

The idea was crazy, but it was the only one we had. Before I knew it, Desmond and I were making our very own cat costumes. We used some old Halloween costumes, leftover craft supplies, and some pajamas I didn't wear anymore.

Zax helped us with the sewing. He's my ghost. And yes, I know it's not exactly normal to have a ghost, but this is Kersville. Having a ghost isn't really all that strange.

"And we're done with the first one," Zax announced. He held up one of the cat costumes.

"Whoa, that looks pretty good,"
I told him. "How did you learn how
to sew? I mean, ghosts don't need
clothes."

"There are a lot of things I can do," Zax responded, smiling proudly. "But here's a ghost secret: I don't ever have to worry about pricking my finger with the needle. I don't even have fingers!"

I'm not going to lie—that kind of blew my mind.

It didn't take long for Zax to fin-
ish both costumes. Desmond and I
put them on, and we looked like real
cats—*giant* cats!

On the way to the pound, I asked Desmond, "Even if the dogs see us, how are we going to get them outside? Isn't the pound like dog jail? They're probably behind bars."

Desmond looked at me with the saddest expression on his face and said, "I hope not."

Then he started to walk faster. Sure, Desmond always had a plan, but this time his brain was probably too filled with puppy-dog wishes. If he had his way, he would bring *all* those dogs home with him!

When we got there, we stood out-side for a few minutes. We were just two giant cats standing in front of a dog pound. Nothing strange about that, right?

"Have you figured out a plan yet?" I asked Desmond. "We can't just walk inside and ask for a puppy prison break."

"I know," Desmond said. "But there has to be a way." Suddenly, a bright light beamed down on us. We froze, thinking we might have set off an alarm or something. It was like a spotlight found us!

SVILLE

POUND

Then we looked up. It was only the moon, and it was full, just like the dogcatcher had told us. In fact, it was the fullest full moon I had ever seen.

I swallowed hard, fear fluttering around in my stomach.

"Why don't we just get out of here before anything weird happens?" I asked. "What if someone sees us dressed like this and puts us in the *cat* pound?"

Desmond looked at me and shook his head like I was being silly. "Don't worry, Andres, moonlight never hurt anyone."

Then we heard something. It was a sound I'll never forget. It made the fear in my stomach stop fluttering and start *flapping*!

The howling had begun.

AAWWW-WOOOO!

CHAPTER SIX

A Howling Good Time

"W-what is happening, Desmond?" I yelled.

He was too busy looking around to answer me. The howling had to be coming from somewhere close. Then we figured it out and looked at each other.

The howling was coming from inside the pound!

My eyes opened wide. I was ready to run away, but Desmond grabbed my tail. He put his finger to his lips and whispered, "Shhh."

Desmond and I tiptoed quietly toward a window at the side of the pound. We peeked inside, and I couldn't believe what I was seeing. Talk about weird!

The dogcatcher was standing with his back to the window. All the dogs were there too, but they weren't locked up. Instead, they were happily watching the dogcatcher. We could tell because they all wagged their tails, which was how dogs smile.

But, that wasn't the weird part.

The dogs weren't the ones howling.

It was the dogcatcher!

Desmond and I looked at each other. Neither of us knew what was going on.

Only one thing was clear: Those dogs really loved the dogcatcher.

They were sending out so much joy that I almost became a dog person.

"See, Desmond," I whispered. "We got it all wrong. The dogs like it here. That dogcatcher must be really nice to them."

Desmond didn't say anything, but the look on his face told me he was thinking. I know he didn't like the dogcatcher. He thought there was something strange about him. But we had to believe what we were seeing.

Maybe the dogcatcher *was* just a good guy who liked taking care of dogs.

That was when the dogcatcher turned around, and it took every bit of courage inside of me not to scream. Even Desmond looked terrified, and he's the bravest kid I know.

The dogcatcher had changed. He was now more like . . . *a dog*! He had hairy arms, a furry face, and a long snout with a nose that sniffed the air.

Then the dogcatcher's glowing eyes fell on us, and I gasped.

The beast let out a loud, chilling howl that echoed through the night.

"Okay," I said as I shut my eyes as tight as I could. "So, the dogcatcher is a werewolf, and we're dressed up like cats. Why don't we head home before this night gets worse?"

"Um, Andres," said Desmond. "It just got worse."

I opened my eyes, and the werewolf was still there. Only now, he was opening the back door to the pound and coming outside to get us.

"Time to run?" I asked.

Desmond nodded and screamed, "BIG-TIME!"

CHAPTER SEVEN

All Bite, No Bark

As I said before, there are dog people, and there are cat people.

But are there *werewolf* people in the world?

I mean, not people who *turn into* werewolves. But I wondered if there were people who *liked* werewolves.

Are there kids who come home from school and can't wait to play with their pet werewolf?

Do they have parents who laugh about the way their werewolf ruins clothes every time they transform?

Are there people who just *love* the way werewolves keep everyone up at night by howling at the moon?

I didn't think so!

Anyway, who had time to think of all that when we were running for our lives?

Dressed as cats.

With a pack of dogs and a real werewolf right behind us.

I mean, even Desmond's stray puppy from the park was after us! How did we end up in this situation?

At least the dogs were quiet. I always thought dogs were supposed to bark at cats, but not *these* dogs. Instead, they were silently chasing us through the streets of Kersville.

Wait, maybe if they were barking, someone would have noticed.

Plus, there were so many dogs loose on the streets, how did nobody notice! Where was the dogcatcher when you really needed him?

Oh yeah, that's right. He was a werewolf, and he was chasing us too!

Ever since I moved to Kersville, I've had to run away from a lot of really weird things: mummies, mer-surfers, zombie zookeepers—you name it!

But dogs are different. They're *fast*! I mean, they have four legs, and I've got only two. There's no way to compete with that.

Desmond and I had a head start, but the pack was catching up to us.

There was nowhere to go. No chance to escape. The Ghost Patrol was doomed!

But then, as we rounded a corner, a door to a store opened up, and
something pulled Desmond and me
inside.

It was Zax. I had never been so happy to see a ghost in my whole life!

The dogs and the werewolf turned the corner and flew right by the store. We could even see the werewolf's shiny, pointy teeth through the front window.

Zax locked the door, and I tried to catch my breath.

Sure, that werewolf was really friendly to the dogs, but I didn't know why he was chasing us.

And I didn't want to find out!

CHAPTER EIGHT

FLEAS, PLEASE!

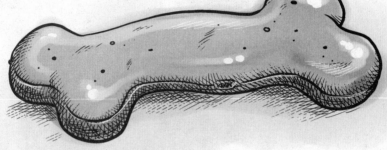

I was shaking. I was scared. Our close call with the werewolf made me want to curl up into a ball and hide.

Even Desmond looked a bit more worried than I'd seen before.

And do you think that stopped Zax from laughing at us?

Absolutely not—he was cracking up! And if you've never heard a ghost laugh, well, you're lucky!

"This isn't funny, Zax," I said. I didn't want to be mad at him, because he saved us, but I couldn't help it.

Zax pulled out a mirror and held it in front of me.

"Oh," I said, seeing myself in the cat costume. I looked at Desmond, and we both smiled. "I guess we do look really silly."

Suddenly, we were all laughing, and I started to calm down.

Desmond and I took off our cat costumes and thanked Zax for saving our lives.

"What were you doing out here?" Desmond asked.

"I was buying these." Zax held up two cat collars with little bells on them. "They were supposed to be for your costumes, but I guess you don't need them. Those dogs totally thought you were cats!"

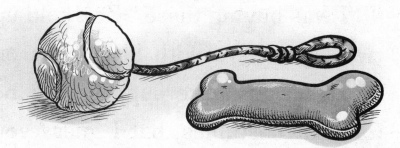

"Wait, what kind of store is this?" Desmond looked around. The walls were filled with chewy balls, rubber bones, pull-ropes, plastic squeakers, doggy treats, and more. Zax had pulled us into a pet shop!

This store was a doggy dreamland!

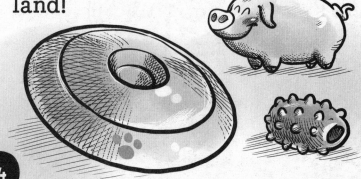

Desmond grabbed some dog toys from the wall and said, "Andres, are you thinking what I'm thinking?"

Here's a tip: If Desmond Cole ever asks you a question like that, let me tell you, the answer is always *no*.

Always!

CHAPTER NINE

PLAY FETCH

Desmond and I loaded up all the doggy toys we could carry while Zax paid for everything. I really don't know how ghosts get money, but Zax had a lot of it.

Anyway, we had to find that pack . . . and it didn't take us long.

They were at the dog park, of course. It looked like they were having a dog-tastic time!

"Maybe we should leave them alone," I whispered to Desmond. "Look at how much fun they're having."

Desmond's puppy was rolling around in the grass, having a blast with some of the other dogs.

Desmond whispered back, "Sure, they're having fun, but we need to find out what this werewolf wants. Follow me."

Then Desmond and I did the unthinkable. We walked right into the dog park. The moonlight was so bright that it looked like daytime. Of course, that didn't help me feel any less afraid. My legs wobbled more and more like taffy with each step.

The dogs stopped playing when they saw us. They sat quietly as the werewolf stalked to the front of the pack.

"*Now* can we leave?" I whimpered as the werewolf inched closer.

"Not yet," Desmond replied. "I need to know what's going on."

Why does he always need to know things?

That was when the werewolf started to sniff the air around us. Desmond and I kept as still as we possibly could.

Desmond slowly said, "Good boy. Good boy. We brought you some toys."

Desmond squeezed a toy, and a loud squeak rang out in the night.

I gulped, waiting for whatever the werewolf was going to do next.

And what he did was . . . smile!

"Toys?" the werewolf asked with
a low growl.

Desmond held up a squeaker ball,
squeezed it again, and a high-pitched
squeak squealed. The werewolf's
tail started to wag wildly.

Desmond threw the ball, and the werewolf darted after it.

I started throwing toys in the other direction. While the werewolf chased Desmond's ball, the rest of the dogs chased my toys . . . right out of the dog park and into an empty playground!

I closed a gate behind them. They would be safe there for now, but Desmond and I still had a werewolf to deal with!

The werewolf came bounding happily back to Desmond holding the ball in his jaws. He dropped it and looked around.

"Wait, where did my pack go?" he asked.

"They're all safe," Desmond told him. "Now it's time for us to talk. What are you up to, werewolf?"

The werewolf glared at us.

"If I tell you," he began, "will you bring the dogs back?"

Desmond nodded. "It's a deal."

And let me tell you that I wasn't prepared for what happened next, which is saying a lot when you live in Kersville.

CHAPTER TEN

PUPPY PALS

A familiar song echoed through the park. I knew it by heart. It was the ice-cream truck!

"Before I start, would you like a frozen treat?" the werewolf asked us. "My friend owns the truck, and I'm really hungry."

The Itsy-Bitsy Ice Cream truck rolled up by the dog park, and its side window slid open.

"Hi, John. I've got your frozen bones," said the ice-cream driver. Then he said, "Oh, you have friends."

"Thanks, Anthony," growled the werewolf. "Will you give these two anything they want?"

Wait, did that werewolf just say *anything they want*?

After Desmond and I let the dogs back into the dog park, we ate ice cream and listened to John the werewolf as he talked about his life.

"It's hard to make friends as a werewolf," he said. "People are too scared, cats are too scared, and even lions at the zoo are too scared."

"You got that right," I told him.
Then John the werewolf howled.

"Sorry, it's a habit. Anyway, I spent a long time looking for friends, until I realized something. Who loves you no matter what? I mean, other than your family."

Maybe the ice cream was clouding my mind, but I couldn't think of anyone.

But Desmond knew right away. "Dogs!" he said. "Dogs love everyone!"

"That's right!" snarled John the werewolf. "So I became an animal control officer—um, we're not called 'dogcatcher' anymore. Now, before every full moon, I round up as many dogs as possible, and we hang out all night."

I had to admit that it *was* kind of brilliant. I guess dogs don't ever judge people *or* werewolves. Then, once the werewolf was friends with the dogs, other dog people—like Anthony—became friends with John too!

So that night we played with the
pups, and it was amazing. Desmond
was as happy as a kid with a million
dogs could be! And me? I had my
ice cream!

Now, every time there's a full moon, John lets us join the pack as honorary members. Not only that—he lets us help out at the pound, too. Or actually it's called the shelter. Desmond loves it!

And me? Okay. Maybe, just maybe, I'm becoming a dog person. I mean, they're all *so* cute! I even think Desmond's puppy is adorable in his own way.

But don't worry. I'll probably never ever *ever* become a werewolf person, except for maybe once in a full moon.